MARTA!
BIG & SMALL

Jen Arena

ILLUSTRATED BY

Angela Dominguez

ROARING BROOK PRESS
New York

Marta is una niña . . .

. . . an ordinary girl.

To a bug, Marta is grande.
Big, very big.

To an elephant,
Marta is PEQUEÑA.
Small, very small.

To a horse,
Marta is Lenta.

Slow, very slow.

To a turtle, Marta is rápida.

Fast, very fast.

To a lion,
Marta is tranQuiLa.
Quiet, very quiet.

To a rabbit, Marta is ruidosa.

Loud,
very loud.

To a snake,
Marta is SABROSA.

Tasty,

very tasty . . .

Marta?

Phew!

Marta is *ingeniosa*.
Clever, very clever.

Marta is loud like EL LeÓn,

quiet like EL conejo,

fast like EL caballo,

slow like
La tortuga,

big like
eL eLefante,

small like *eL insecto.*

And clever, very clever,
like una niña.

MARTA is . . .

una niña – a girl

grande – big

pequeña – small

lenta – slow

rápida – fast

tranquila – quiet

ruidosa – loud

sabrosa – tasty

ingeniosa – clever

MARTA meets . . .

el insecto — the bug

el elefante — the elephant

el caballo — the horse

la tortuga — the turtle

el león — the lion

el conejo — the rabbit

la serpiente — the snake

For Dario, without you there would be no Marta.
Gracias, mi querido esposo. —J.A.

To Connie, Jen, Linda, and my family of course. —A.D.

Text copyright © 2016 by Jennifer Arena
Illustrations © 2016 by Angela Dominguez
Published by Roaring Brook Press
Roaring Brook Press is a division of
Holtzbrinck Publishing Holdings Limited Partnership
120 Broadway, New York, NY 10271
mackids.com

Library of Congress Cataloging-in-Publication Data
Arena, Jen, author.
    Marta! big & small / by Jen Arena ; illustrated by Angela Dominguez. — First edition.
        pages cm
    Summary: In this story that incorporates Spanish words, Marta explores the world of
opposites and animals.
    ISBN 978-1-62672-243-9 (hardcover)
    1. Polarity—Juvenile fiction.   2. Animals—Juvenile fiction.   [1. English language—
Synonyms and antonyms—Fiction.   2. Animals—Fiction.   3. Hispanic Americans—
Fiction.   4. Spanish language—Vocabulary—Fiction.]   I. Dominguez, Angela N.,
illustrator.   II. Title.   III. Title: Marta! big and small.

PZ7.A6826Mar 2016
[E]—dc23
                                                                                                      2015013769

Our books may be purchased in bulk for promotional, educational, or business use. Please
contact your local bookseller or the Macmillan Corporate and Premium Sales Department
at (800) 221-7945 ext. 5442 or by e-mail at MacmillanSpecialMarkets@macmillan.com.

First edition 2016
Book design by Kristie Radwilowicz
Color separations by Embassy Graphics
Printed in China by Toppan Leefung Printing Ltd., Dongguan City, Guangdong Province

5   7   9   10   8   6